The DINOSAUR TAMER

illustrated by

CAROL GREATHOUSE · JOHN SHROADES

DUTTON CHILDREN'S BOOKS

DUTTON CHILDREN'S BOOKS
A division of Penguin Young Readers Group

Published by the Penguin Group
Penguin Group (USA) Inc., 375 Hudson Street, New York, New York 10014, U.S.A. • Penguin Group (Canada), 90 Eglinton
Avenue East, Suite 700, Toronto, Ontario M4P 2Y3, Canada (a division of Pearson Penguin Canada Inc.) • Penguin Books
Ltd, 80 Strand, London WC2R 0RL, England • Penguin Ireland, 25 St Stephen's Green, Dublin 2, Ireland (a division of
Penguin Books Ltd) • Penguin Group (Australia), 250 Camberwell Road, Camberwell, Victoria 3124, Australia (a division
of Pearson Australia Group Pty Ltd) • Penguin Books India Pvt Ltd, 11 Community Centre, Panchsheel Park, New Delhi—
110 017, India • Penguin Group (NZ), 67 Apollo Drive, Rosedale, North Shore 0632, New Zealand (a division of Pearson New
Zealand Ltd) • Penguin Books (South Africa) (Pty) Ltd, 24 Sturdee Avenue, Rosebank, Johannesburg 2196, South Africa •
Penguin Books Ltd, Registered Offices: 80 Strand, London WC2R 0RL, England

CIP Data is available.

Published in the United States by Dutton Children's Books,
a division of Penguin Young Readers Group
345 Hudson Street, New York, New York 10014
www.penguin.com/youngreaders

Designed by Jason Henry
Manufactured in China • First Edition
ISBN: 978-0-525-47866-9
10 9 8 7 6 5 4 3 2 1

To my own Dinosaur Tamers: Walter, Daniel,
Mark, Jonathan, Violet, Evelyn, and Ruby.
Ride 'em cowboy!
C.G.

To Mom and Dad
J.S.

Back when the old, old West was still as green as a bristlecone pine and cowboys were as common as warts on a *Stegosaurus*, one cowboy stood out among all cowboys. He was as strong as an *Iguanodon* and as fast as a *Utah Raptor*, and his name was Rocky.

Now, Rocky weren't a big feller, but his size didn't matter.

From the time he was a babe in his cradle, there was somethin' different about him.

He teethed on a *Deinonychus* femur and used an *Ankylosaurus* tail as a rattle.

By the time he was knee-high to a *Pterodactyl* egg, he could rope a *Stegosaurus* at ninety paces while wearin' a blindfold and eatin' a prickly pear.

Once, when he was late for supper, he harnessed himself to the meanest ole *plesiosaurus* that ever swam the Great Salt Lake. He got back to shore quicker than a warthog can say "ugly." Without a doubt, he was the greatest dinosaur tamer ever.

Kids dreamed of growin' up to be a dinosaur tamer, just like Rocky. And whenever there was a dinosaur problem, they took to calling him.

Until one day when the greatest dinosaur problem of all arrived in the form of the roughest, the toughest, the most ferocious dinosaur to ever kick dirt: T. Rex.

T. Rex was so tough he scratched his itches in the giant saguaro cactus forest and drank his water straight from Arkansas's Hot Springs. *Yaaaahwza!* T. Rex was so mean a family of possums once threw up their paws and surrendered without a peep. Lucky for them, T. Rex had just finished a big meal.

He was the rip-roarin'est, snip-snortin'est reptilian that ever did stomp the earth. And he would not quit pestering the townsfolk.

One day after T. Rex chased the kids' saber kitten up a tree and swiped the johnnycakes off the fire, folks had had enough. "Something has to be done," they grumbled. Didn't take no time at all to decide Rocky was their man. Problem was, Rocky was on the annual sauropod roundup. So they threw some wood on the fire to signal him.

After the smoke cleared, they beat out his number on the bongo drums. *Boom-ba-de-dum. Boom-boom-ba-de-dum.* Before the last *de-dum* faded into the hills, Rocky swooped in ridin' a slobberin' saber-toothed tiger and leadin' a pack train of *Pachycephalosaurus*.

"That the *Tyrannosaurus* rex you're meanin' me to tame?" Rocky asked.

"That's him all right," said the mayor. "He's the rip-roarin'est, snip-snortin'est reptilian—"

Rocky held up his hand. "Time's a wastin'," he said. He whistled for his *Pachycephalosaurus* and began to uncoil his genuine crocodile-hide lariat. Fifty feet...one hundred feet...three hundred feet...one thousand feet.

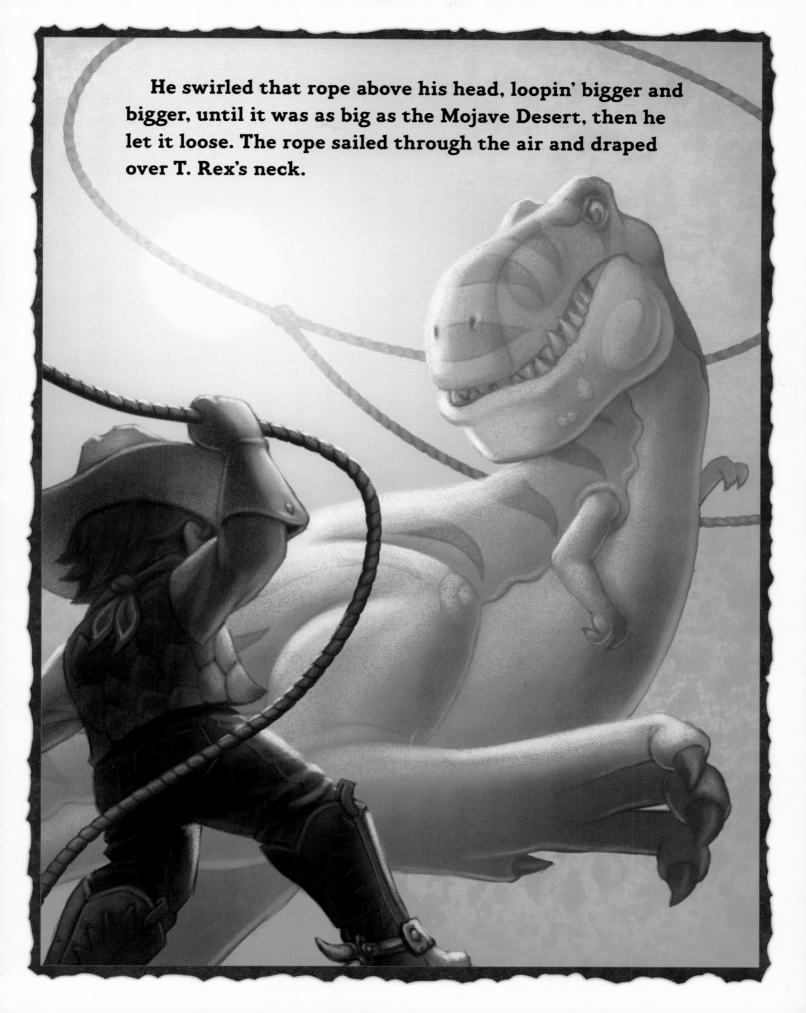

He swirled that rope above his head, loopin' bigger and bigger, until it was as big as the Mojave Desert, then he let it loose. The rope sailed through the air and draped over T. Rex's neck.

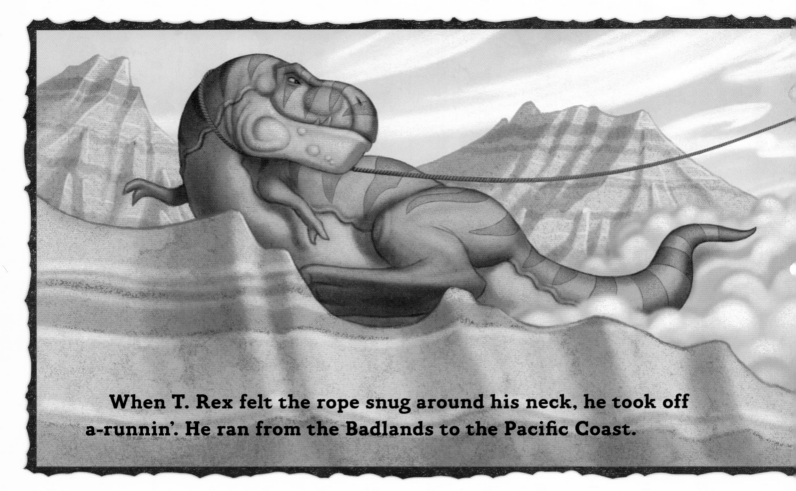

When T. Rex felt the rope snug around his neck, he took off a-runnin'. He ran from the Badlands to the Pacific Coast.

Then he circled 'round, dodged through some ponderosa pines, and ran for the Olympic rain forests.

When he hit Yellowstone, he was goin' seventy miles per hour and sidesteppin' geysers with Rocky bumpin' along behind him. Before he slowed down, T. Rex had covered fifteen states and visited three national parks.

If Rocky ever had a second thought about tanglin' with T. Rex, he didn't say. He just hung on for dear life. Finally, Rocky got hold of a hill and dallied that rope 'round and 'round until T. Rex had nowhere to run. T. Rex kept workin' back and forth, back and forth, until he'd whittled that hill into a pile of rocks.

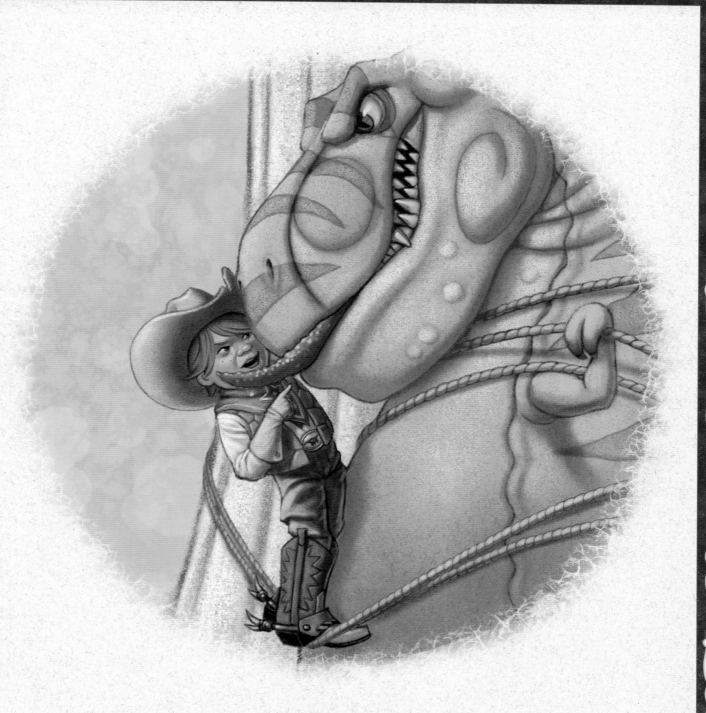

T. Rex wound himself so tight, he couldn't move.
Rocky stepped up and looked at him eye to eye, snout
to nose. "I mean to break you," he said. T. Rex gave a
toothy grin and flicked his rough tongue across Rocky's
cheek. Then, just to let Rocky know he wasn't tamed yet,
he let out a low rumble.

Rocky crept up to T. Rex, unwound the rope, and threw one leg up over that ugly, green hide. "Git up," Rocky yelled, and jabbed T. Rex in the ribs with his boar-tooth spurs. T. Rex let out a beller that was heard from the Rio Grande to the Columbia River Gorge. The sound split the earth right where he stood.

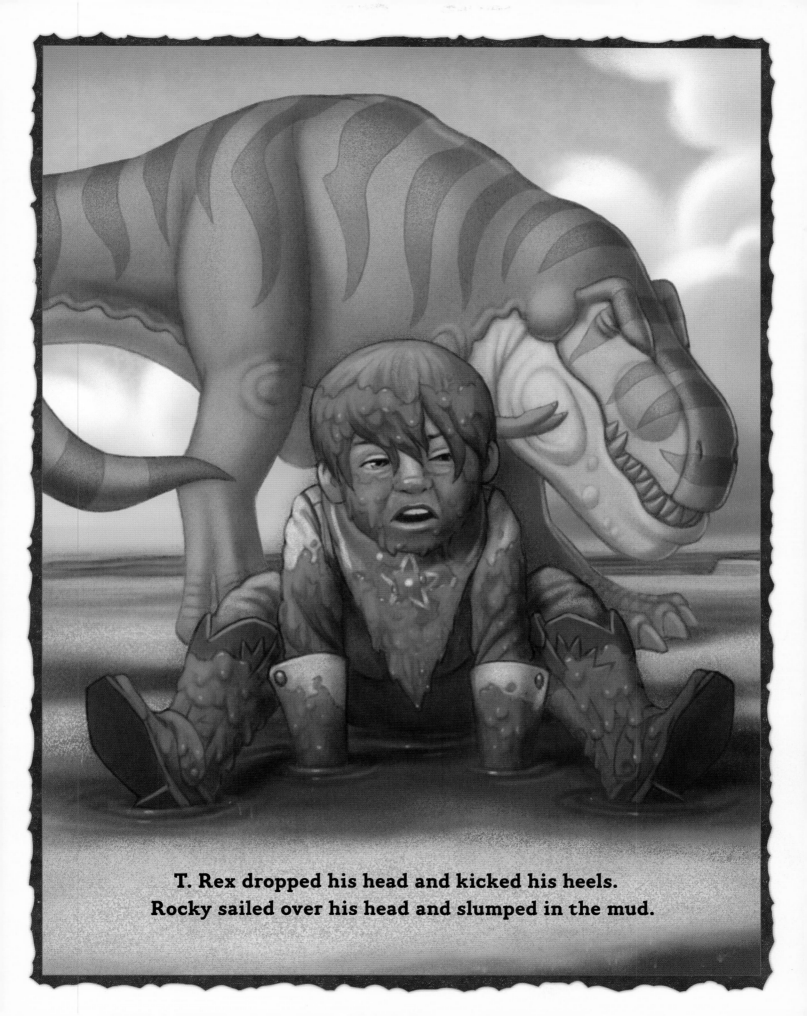

T. Rex dropped his head and kicked his heels.
Rocky sailed over his head and slumped in the mud.

"Well, I'll be," Rocky sputtered. He shook himself off and rubbed his bad hip. There was no way T. Rex was lettin' him back on. When Rocky circled left, T. Rex circled right. There was a half sashay and what looked like a do-si-do before the dinosaur dance ended. While T. Rex was concentrating on the dance steps, Rocky crept up beside him and hopped on.

The moment Rocky landed, T. Rex threw his head down and slammed his tail around. He spun to the left, then he spun to the right. He kept wallerin' back and forth tryin' to dislodge that varmint on his back. Pretty soon his wallerin' had created quite a hole.

When T. Rex found he couldn't throw Rocky off his back, he took to snarlin' and snappin' his teeth. Rocky just hunkered down for the ride. "YEEEEHOOOSAPHAT," he yelled. "Hot diggity dino!"

Whichever way T. Rex bit, Rocky dodged the other way. T. Rex couldn't get ahold of him. Finally, T. Rex was puffin' so hard, he couldn't go on. He was so tuckered out, his tail dragged behind him, slicing through the silt.

By now, T. Rex couldn't have mustered up a Texas two-step let alone another chase. Rocky reached forward and patted the green-hided monster. "Attaboy," he said. Then he pulled a zucchini out of his hat and offered it to T. Rex.

While T. Rex gnawed on the zucchini, Rocky sang a little tune into his leathery ear. When he was done, T. Rex was as docile as a fresh-hatched platypus pup.

Olympic rain forest

WASHINGTON

OREGON

IDAHO

MONTANA

NORTH DAKOTA

Crater Lake

Devil's Tower

SOUTH DAKOTA

Badlands

Yellowstone

WYOMING

NEVADA

Great Salt Lake

NEBRASKA

Pacific Coast

Ponderosa pines

UTAH

COLORADO

KANSAS

Great Valley
Western Foothills

CALIFORNIA

Grand Canyon

Mojave Desert

ARIZONA

NEW MEXICO

OKLAHOMA

Giant saguaro cactus forest

PACIFIC OCEAN

TEXAS

MEXICO

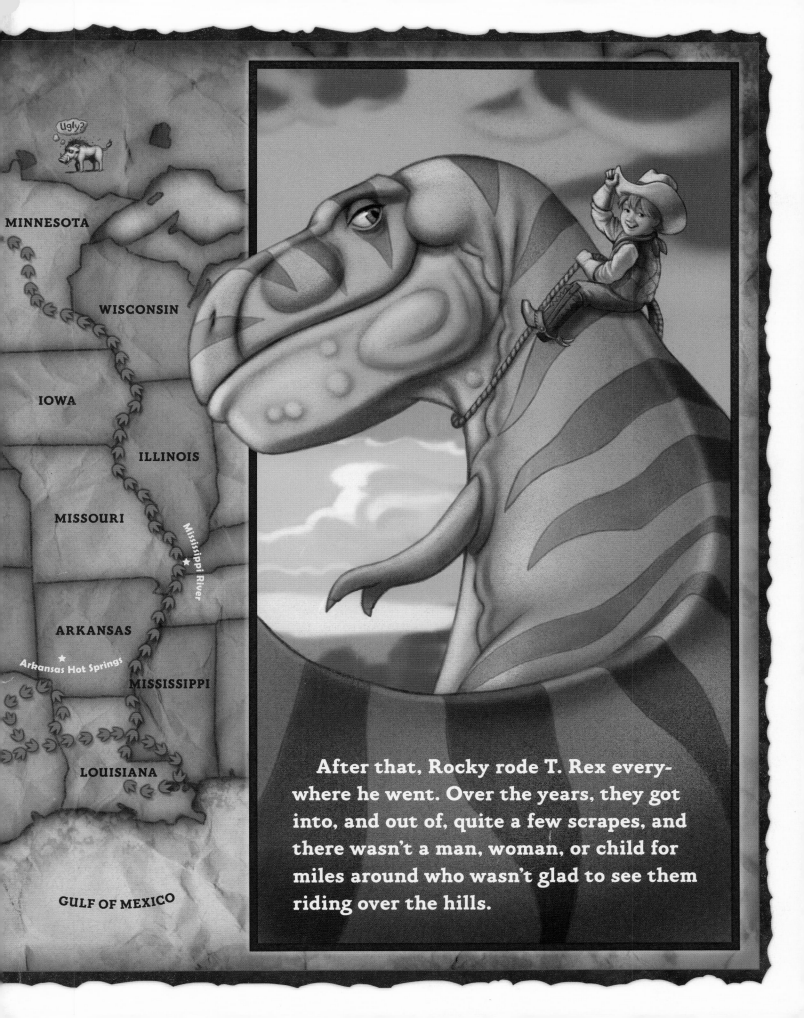

After that, Rocky rode T. Rex every-where he went. Over the years, they got into, and out of, quite a few scrapes, and there wasn't a man, woman, or child for miles around who wasn't glad to see them riding over the hills.

Folks all remembered how Rocky and T. Rex teamed up, but no one knows what finally became of them. There are a handful of folks who claim Rocky and T. Rex still roam the western foothills. They say when the sun dips just right in the afternoon sky, they can still see the shadow of Rocky and his dinosaur standing tall and proud.